A PHONY LINCOLN

In our cart were a container of milk, a container of juice, chocolate-chip cookies, donuts with chocolate sprinkles, chocolate-covered donuts, a bag of chocolate chips, and gumdrops.

Mr. Edwards rang up everything and put it all into two shopping bags. Sara gave him two five-dollar bills. He started to put the bills into the cash register drawer and then he stopped. He looked at Sara, at me, and then at one of the bills. "I can't take this," he said. "It's counterfeit."

T. F. BENSON AND THE DINOSAUR MADNESS
  MYSTERY by David A. Adler

BE A PERFECT PERSON IN JUST THREE DAYS!
  by Stephen Manes

BIG RED by Jim Kjelgaard

ENCYCLOPEDIA BROWN BOY DETECTIVE
  by Donald Sobel

THE EYES OF THE KILLER ROBOT by John
  Bellairs

THE GLOVE OF DARTH VADER (Star Wars #1)
  by Paul Davids and Hollace Davids

SEAL CHILD by Sylvia Peck

THEY'RE TORTURING TEACHERS IN ROOM
  104 by Jerry Piasecki

A VAMPIRE NAMED MURRAY by Judi Miller

T. F. Benson and the Funny-Money Mystery

by David A. Adler

A BANTAM SKYLARK BOOK
NEW YORK · TORONTO · LONDON · SYDNEY · AUCKLAND

This book is for my son, Michael Seth,
whose constant complaints that I'm too
friendly inspired this series.

RL 4, 008–012

T. F. BENSON AND THE FUNNY-MONEY MYSTERY
A Bantam Skylark Book / November 1992

Skylark Books is a registered trademark of Bantam Books,
a division of Bantam Doubleday Dell Publishing Group, Inc.
Registered in U.S. Patent and Trademark Office and elsewhere.

ISBN 0-553-15979-8

Published simultaneously in the United States and Canada

Bantam Books are published by Bantam Books, a division of Bantam
Doubleday Dell Publishing Group, Inc. Its trademark, consisting of the
words "Bantam Books" and the portrayal of a rooster, is Registered
in U.S. Patent and Trademark Office and in other countries. Marca
Registrada. Bantam Books, 666 Fifth Avenue, New York, New York
10103.

PRINTED IN THE UNITED STATES OF AMERICA

CWO   0 9 8 7 6 5 4 3 2 1

Contents

1. A Yellow Shoe!

I sat by the window and watched the moving men unload the truck. First they took out the usual stuff: beds, chairs, tables, and a couch. You can tell a lot about people by the furniture they have. This stuff was mostly made of wood and covered in dark cloth, so I was sure the people moving into apartment 3D were old.

Next the men took out a standing lamp. The shade was yellow, with fringes. Then the men carried cardboard boxes from the truck. On the side of each box was a label. I yawned. The people moving into 3D were definitely old and boring. Anyone who puts labels on boxes has no sense of adventure. What fun is opening a box if you know what's inside?

I had hoped someone exciting would move in, like an old sea captain with a cursing parrot or a sailor with Mandy G. tattooed on his arm. Mandy G. had left him and he was stuck with the tattoo. For the last thirty-eight years he had been searching for another woman named Mandy G.

"T.F.," my mother called. "Come here and try on some clothes."

My real name is Brian Benson, but T.F. is my nickname. It stands "Too friendly," which my parents and friends started calling me because I'll talk to anyone. Once I even talked to a statue—it looked real.

"T.F., I'm waiting."

Mom and my brother, Jeffrey, were in my room. Mom was sitting on my bed next to a pile of clothes. School starts in two weeks, and she always buys me clothes before school. Jeffrey was hopping around my room wearing my baseball glove and one of my shirts. He looked weird. He's only five, and the shirt hung all the way down to his ankles. He looked up at me and smiled.

I said, "You look good, Jeffrey."

"I know."

My mother handed me a yellow long-sleeved shirt. I put it on over my T-shirt and tucked it into my pants.

"Wouldn't it be great, Mom, if an old baseball

coach moved into 3D?" I asked. "Great players would still come to him for tips on batting, even though he was too old to coach. They'd line up in the hall, and while they waited to talk to the coach, they'd give me autographed baseballs and free tickets to games."

"T.F., will you take me to the baseball games?"

"Sure, Jeffrey. Mom, would an old baseball coach have a yellow lamp shade with fringes?"

"I don't know," she said.

"Would a sailor?"

Mom didn't answer. Instead she gave me a red-and-black-checkered shirt to try on.

"Would a sea captain put labels on his boxes?"

Mom said, "That shirt fits nicely. I should have bought the green-and-black one, too."

"Nah," I said, "a sea captain would move in with a few duffel bags, maybe a trunk, a numbered buoy, and a life preserver."

"Don't take off that shirt. Try this sweater on over it."

I pulled the sweater over my head and thought about the labels again. 3D was definitely someone who was neat and organized. An old account-ant or a math teacher like my mom was moving in.

Mom gave me a pair of black pants. I put them on in the bathroom. It wasn't easy wearing them back to my room. The legs were way too long, and I had to hold them up around my waist.

"Look, look, T.F.," Jeffrey called, "a yellow shoe!"

Through the window of my room I saw the moving men take a huge yellow shoe from the truck. I couldn't believe it. The shoe was as big as our kitchen table. I ran to the window and let go of my pants. They dropped for a second. Jeffrey pointed at me and laughed, and my mother said, "That reminds me. You'll need new underwear for school, too."

I pulled up my pants and watched the men carry the shoe into the building.

"Mom, why would an accountant need a big yellow shoe?"

"Maybe he has a big yellow foot."

"No, Mom, this shoe is huge. It took two men to carry it."

My mother got off the bed and stood next to Jeffrey and me by the window. We watched the men go back to the truck. They came out carrying a great big orange derby.

"Who would wear a hat that color?" Mom asked.

"Who would wear a hat that big?" I wanted to know.

One of the men said something. It must have been, "I can take this myself," because then he bent down and got under the hat. He stood inside, reached out, and held on to the brim.

Jeffrey laughed and said, "It's a walking hat."

Mom and I laughed, too.

The orange derby walked toward the door of the building, but obviously the man inside couldn't see. The hat bumped into a bush. It turned and hit a tree. It turned again and hit the truck. The other man watched and laughed until the hat walked toward the street. Then he came and helped carry it into the building.

A yellow shoe! An orange hat! 3D may label his boxes, but he didn't seem boring anymore.

"Hey, Mom," I asked, "do you think whoever is moving into 3D is here already?"

"Hm, yes. They're probably in the apartment telling the movers where to put everything."

I left the window and walked toward the door. "Where are you going?" Mom asked.

"To meet 3D."

"You're not going anywhere until after you finish trying on these clothes. And you're not bothering people on their first day here."

I tried on six more shirts and three more pairs of pants.

My mother loves to shop, but all I care about is finding something to wear when I open my closet. I don't care if what I wear matches, but Mom surely does.

While I tried on the clothes, I kept watching through the window. The moving men brought in a dark wood table with lots of carvings, a large bookcase with glass doors, a huge bow tie, and two purple doors with stars, moons, and planets painted on.

This was weird stuff. I wanted to meet 3D.

"Pow! Pow! Squeak! Help!"

Jeffrey was watching television in the living room, but Mom didn't notice. She was too busy with my clothing. It was a good thing, because she doesn't approve of the cartoons Jeffrey likes. She says they're too violent. But Dad says watching a mouse hit a cat with a huge hammer might teach him to stick up for himself.

"Bam! Bam! Bam!"

I took off a shirt with red stripes, and Mom said, "That's it." She pointed to the pile of clothes closest to her and said, "I'm keeping these. Is that okay?"

"Sure."

"Don't you want to look at them?"

I looked at them.

"And I'm returning these."

I looked at the other pile. Both piles looked the same to me.

While I tied my sneakers, Mom took the return pile from my room. I had finished tying my right sneaker and was looping the laces on my left when Mom poked her head back into my room and said, "Don't annoy the new people."

I told her, "I'm going outside."

I said good-bye to Jeffrey, but he didn't hear me. He was watching a mouse pour wet cement on a sleeping cat's tail.

The elevator was waiting at our floor. I decided to race it down. I stuck my hand inside the car, pressed 1, and ran to the stairs. We live on the fifth floor, and I can usually beat the elevator to the lobby. I raced past the fourth-floor door and then past the third. But halfway to the second I stopped. Maybe the new tenant in 3D is lonely, I thought, and is wondering where all the people living in the building are hiding. Maybe just what he needs is to meet someone friendly, someone to welcome him to his new home.

Mom had told me not to annoy 3D, and I wouldn't. I would just tell the person that I often do odd jobs for the building's superintendent. That way the new tenant would know to call on me if he ever needed anything. I wouldn't annoy him. I'd just be there if he needed me.

2. Dangerous Pets

I climbed back up the few stairs to the third floor. I opened the door and looked down the hall. There were boxes in front of 3D. I saw the two moving men leave the apartment and walk to the elevator. Then an old woman came out, the fringed lampshade type.

The woman looked at the label on one of the boxes and called inside the apartment. A girl about my age, twelve, came out. She had long blond hair and was wearing green plaid shorts, a blue-striped shirt, and socks that didn't match. I don't mean they didn't match the shorts or the shirt. They didn't match each other. One sock was red and the other was white. This girl was the orange-derby type, definitely.

The girl and the old woman began to lift one of the boxes. Then the girl looked up. She saw me, and before I knew it, she was walking toward me. It was weird. She didn't smile. She just looked straight at me and walked.

"You're probably wondering who we are, why we moved here, and if we have dangerous pets," she said. "Help me carry a few boxes, and I'll tell you everything."

Dangerous pets!

She told me her name was Sara Bell, and that it rhymes with Clarabell, the clown on the *Howdy Doody Show*. I had never heard of the clown or the show, but Sara said, "Ask your parents." Maybe I will, I thought.

I found out that Sara is artistic. She made the shoes, hat, and bow tie out of papier mâché when she was in her "clothing" period. Now she's in her "purple door" period. "I don't think I'll stay too long with purple doors," she said. "They're kind of limiting."

Sara talked a lot and she talked really fast. I didn't understand most of what she said, but I didn't want to interrupt her. I just listened.

While we were unpacking, Sara introduced me to Grams. That's what she calls her grandmother.

Sara has lived with Grams since she was ten—since Sara was ten, not Grams. Sara said, "Don't ask me to tell you about my parents. It's a depressing story, and I don't want to depress the only neighbor to help us on our first day here."

Grams was really nice. When I told her that Sara's clothes clashed, Grams whispered to me, "She likes to clash."

It's a good thing my mother doesn't pick out Sara's clothes.

Grams had never been a sea captain, sailor, or baseball coach. But she is a bookkeeper, which is almost the same as an accountant.

"Well," I said, "let me know if you ever need some help here. I'm the super's kid, and I can help you carry groceries, change light bulbs, and even paint closets."

"You're a Super Kid?" Sara said. "Does that mean you can fly or see through walls? Can you bend metal? Could you race against a speeding train and win?" She leaned close to me and whispered, "Are you wearing a disguise under your shirt?"

"No, I'm not a *Super* Kid," I explained. "I'm the super's kid. I help the super, the superintendent of the building. His name is Steve and he's in Fillmore College. When he's not around, I help out. I don't do electrical work. It's too dangerous. And I don't do plumbing, but I do just about everything else." Finally I was getting a chance to talk. "I'm T.F. Benson. My real name is Brian, but people call me T.F. because . . . well . . . anyway, I can't fly."

"But you sure do talk fast!" Sara said. "Remember, a speeding train curdles the milk."

"What?" I asked. Mom would call Sara "unusual." To me she was slightly weird.

Grams asked me, "Why are you called T.F.?"

I told her, "I'm friendly. Some people say I'm too friendly. T.F. stands for Too Friendly."

"Does a Super Kid get paid to help people?" Grams asked.

"Steve gets paid by the owner of the building to keep everything looking and working right. Anyone living here who needs help with other things pays him extra. If Steve can't do the job because he's at school or studying, I do it, and people pay me, too."

"Oh, I thought that when you offered to help us, you were being friendly," Grams said. "I didn't know you wanted to be paid."

"I don't. I mean, I *am* being friendly," I said. "I'm always friendly. I just wanted you to know about me, in case you need some help after you move in and you can't find Steve. Right now, I want to help you, to be friendly. I *don't* want to be paid."

Finally they seemed to get it. After that I

helped them unpack. Sara and I worked for a long time. Grams sat down a lot. Then Sara sat on the couch and said, "I need a rest, too. And anyway, foam wasn't made in a day."

I corrected her. "You mean, 'Rome wasn't built in a day.'"

She shrugged her shoulders and said, "Whatever."

I sat on the chair next to Grams. She took a notepad from her pocket, wrote the date, the time, and what Sara had said, "Foam wasn't made in a day." Then Grams said, "One day I'm going to get this published. I'll call it *Sara's Book of Peculiar Quotations*."

Sara was sitting across from me. She stared at me for a while. I was beginning to feel uncomfortable when she said, "You dress funny. Everything matches."

"I know. My mother hates it when I clash."

Sara threw one of the couch pillows at me and said, "Don't darn the socks. Just let your toes hang out."

"Huh?"

"Be yourself. Be free," she explained.

"Oh."

Sara and Grams told me that before they moved, they had lived about two miles away, in a one-bedroom apartment. They moved because they needed more room. Now they have two bedrooms. They also moved to be closer to the train station. Grams rides the train to work three days a week, and our building is right near the station.

"Do you want something to eat?" Grams asked me.

"I can go to my apartment to eat. I live right upstairs, on the fifth floor."

"No, no, you stay right here," Grams insisted, and brought out a tin of oatmeal cookies. She sat on the chair next to me, broke a cookie into small pieces, and then slowly ate each of the pieces.

"When Grams was young, she was allowed one cookie and milk for a snack before she went to sleep," Sara said.

"We couldn't have more than the one cookie," Grams told me, "but we could have as many crumbs from the bottom of the tin as we wanted. So when my mother left the kitchen, Rae and I would break a cookie and then eat the crumbs."

"Rae is Grams's sister," Sara said.

Grams smiled. She ate a few more small cookie pieces and said, "But my mother knew. Once she wrote us this note and left it in the tin. 'Please don't break these cookies. I'm having guests for tea tomorrow, and I need them all.'"

"Ever since then Grams has liked cookie crumbs," Sara said.

"But not Rae," Grams told me. "Today, if she finds a small crack in a cookie, she won't eat it."

We were all quiet for a while. Then Sara said, "I'm thirsty. Do we have any milk or juice?"

"I haven't shopped yet," Grams said. "Bring me my bag. I'll give you money, and maybe T.F. can take you to the nearest grocery, and you can buy some drinks."

Grams gave Sara some money, and the two of us went to the small grocery near our building. Mr. Edwards, the store owner, was in the fruit-and-vegetable section.

"Hello, T.F."

I introduced him to Sara and told him all about her, Grams, the yellow shoe, and the orange derby. Sara was impatient.

"You can keep talking and talking and talking," she said, "while I do the shopping."

Mr. Edwards has a three-month-old granddaughter. Every time I come into his store he has new photographs of her. I followed him to the cash register, where he showed me about twenty pictures of his granddaughter sleeping in a bassinet. Then he whispered to me, "Your friend's socks are different colors."

"She's artistic," I told him. "Sometimes artists dress like that."

Sara wheeled her shopping cart to the front of the store, where the cash register is.

"Is that what you bought?" I asked.

In the cart was a container of milk, a container of juice, chocolate-chip cookies, donuts with chocolate sprinkles, chocolate-covered donuts, a bag of chocolate chips, and gumdrops.

"You know what old John Paul Jones said, 'Don't give up the chocolate chip.'"

I corrected her again. "He said, 'Don't give up the ship.'"

"Whatever."

Mr. Edwards rang up everything and put it all into two shopping bags. Sara gave him two five-dollar bills. He started to put the bills into the cash-register drawer, and then he stopped. He looked at Sara, at me, and then at one of the bills. "I can't take this," he said. "It's counterfeit."

3. Funny Money

"Here, take a look," Mr. Edwards said.

He showed us the real five-dollar bill and the one he said was counterfeit.

"Look at the green letters on the front of this phony bill," he said. "They're written by hand. And look at President Lincoln's beard. If you look closely at the real bill, you can see separate lines. On the phony bill his beard is fuzzy. The shade of green on the back looks wrong. I think the bill was made on a copying machine. Even the paper doesn't feel right."

Mr. Edwards took out a red marker and made a large X on both sides of the phony bill. "I'm doing this to protect you," he said, "so you don't forget and try to spend it somewhere else. You could get arrested."

Without that bill, Sara didn't have enough money to pay for the groceries. Mr. Edwards said she could take the food home anyway. "I know T.F. and trust him. Just bring the money you owe me the next time you come here."

I carried the bag with the milk and juice. Sara carried the chocolate goodies. We walked quietly for a while. Then Sara sat on the bus-stop bench near our building, put down her bag, and took out the box with the sprinkled donuts. She shook the box hard a few times. I watched as she opened it and poured the loose sprinkles into her hand and ate them. Then she offered me a donut.

"They're bald," I told Sara.

"Just pretend I bought donuts without sprinkles. The cow doesn't jump if her hooves are wet."

"What?"

"The cow doesn't jump if her hooves are wet."

"What does *that* mean?" I asked.

"Nothing. I just didn't know what to say about the sprinkles."

The donut tasted pretty good, even without the sprinkles.

I wanted to talk about the funny money, but I didn't want Sara to think I didn't trust her, or that

I thought she and Grams were criminals or something. I just sat on that bus-stop bench and ate. Halfway through my donut I realized that Sara was looking at me.

She smiled.

I smiled.

"Grams is a bookkeeper," she said.

"I know."

"She works three days a week. Today is not one of her workdays."

"I know."

Sara poured more sprinkles into her hand and then said, "We're not counterfeiters."

"I know that, too."

Poor Sara, I thought. She just moved to a new neighborhood, and now she's afraid that her only friend here thinks she's a criminal. I wanted to let her know that we could be friends. Maybe in two weeks, when school starts, we could walk there together. I could show her around and tell her how to handle the principal. He can be a real pain.

A bus stopped. The door opened. "Well, are you getting on or not?" the driver called.

Sara and I turned to see who he was shouting at.

"I'm talking to you," he snapped.

"Oh!" I ran to the open door of the bus and

told the driver, "We're not going anyplace. We're just sitting on the bench here and talking. We're not waiting for the bus. Sara just moved in and . . ."

The driver closed the door and drove off.

My mother often tells me that sometimes people aren't interested in everything I have to tell them. Sometimes I really am too friendly.

When I came back to the bench, Sara was looking at the phony bill. "Grams must have bought something and was given this in the change instead of real money. It's worthless—and it cost us five dollars."

"Whoever is making and passing those bills is costing a lot of people five dollars," I added. "I'm sure this isn't the only phony bill he or she has made."

Sara looked me right in the eyes. "You're a Super Kid," she said as she stood up. "Can't you stop him? Don't Super Kids stand for peace and justice and the right-of-way?"

"I carry packages. I change light bulbs. I paint closets," I said.

Sara said, "Well, I want to find out how Grams got stuck with this funny money. The first thing we have to do is speak to the victim, my Grams."

We met Steve, the superintendent, in the lobby. He didn't have any work for me, but he said the fall college semester was starting soon. "Then you'll have plenty of jobs, T.F."

I introduced him to Sara, and showed him the counterfeit money. "Look at the green numbers on the bill," I said. "Look at President Lincoln's beard, the fuzzy lines, and feel the paper."

Sara pressed the button for the elevator.

"I don't have to look at Lincoln's beard to know this is a phony," Steve said. "There's a big red X on both sides."

"Mr. Edwards put them there," I explained. "Sara bought some milk and juice and lots of chocolate stuff—chips, and sprinkled donuts. When we tried to pay him with this, he told us it was phony. He didn't want us to forget and try to spend it. You know, we could get arrested for spending counterfeit money."

"T.F.," Sara called, "the elevator is here."

"Sara thinks Grams bought something and someone gave her the bill in the change. It cost her five dollars, you know, because he should have given Grams *real* money."

"T.F., I can't hold these doors forever."

"We're going to find out where Grams got the funny money," I continued.

"I'm letting go of the doors."

I ran to the elevator. After the doors closed,

Sara told me, "You know, you have a problem. You talk too much, and you tell people things they don't want to hear. That's why you talk so fast. You want to say as much as you can before your audience walks off."

I was about to tell Sara that she talks a lot, too, and that she also talks fast, but I didn't. I figured that the best answer to someone who says I talk too much is not to say anything.

We got off the elevator at the third floor. We went to 3D and Sara rang the doorbell. Grams didn't answer. Sara knocked.

"Don't you have a key?"

"Not yet. Grams is getting one made for me." Sara knocked again.

"Maybe she went out," I suggested.

"No. If she did, she would have left a note on the door telling me where she went and when she would be back."

Sara knocked again.

"I'll go downstairs and get Steve. He has a key to every apartment in the building."

Steve came upstairs with a whole ring of keys. It took him awhile to find the one for 3D. When he opened the door, we saw Grams. She was on the floor near the couch. And she was just lying there.

4. More Funny Money

"Grams! Grams," Sara called and ran to her. She held her grandmother's hand. Sara was crying.

"She's breathing," Steve said. "Maybe she fainted."

Sara patted her grandmother's hand. She pushed the hair away from Grams's eyes and gently touched her cheek.

I went to the telephone. "I'm calling for an ambulance," I said, and I dialed 911. The operator asked me our address, if Grams was moving, if there were any sudden shakes, and if we had tried to wake her.

I told her, "She's just lying here on the floor. We came in and found her like this. Please hurry."

It seemed like a long time before the Emergency Medical Service arrived, but it was really just a few minutes. While we waited, Grams moved a little and opened her eyes. She tried to talk, but we couldn't understand her. Steve told her to stay still.

There was a loud knock. I opened the door just a little, and two men in white uniforms with a stretcher on wheels pushed their way inside. One of the paramedics asked questions.

"Did you see her fall?"

"Did you see her shaking?"

"Has she made any sudden movements?"

"Do you know of any illnesses she has?"

"Does she take any medicines?"

Sara answered, "No," after each question.

The other paramedic listened to Grams's breathing, checked her pulse, and held a tube to her mouth to give her oxygen. He did everything real fast, and before I knew it, Grams was on the stretcher and on her way out of the apartment. Sara went with her. Steve and I watched at the window as they wheeled Grams out of the building, into the ambulance, and drove off.

There had been such a commotion, and now it was so quiet. We turned away from the window and looked around the room. It was a mess. Besides all the stuff that hadn't been unpacked yet, pillows were off the couch. The milk, juice, and chocolate goodies had fallen out of the bag. Steve straightened up the room. I put away the groceries.

It was already late in the afternoon. I went to my apartment, to my room. I took out an old baseball magazine. I had looked at it many times before. I turned the pages, but I wasn't really reading. I kept watching out the window, hoping to see Grams and Sara coming back into the building.

I didn't hear Mom call me to dinner until she came to my door and said, "Are you asleep?"

"No, I was just reading."

"Well, we're eating now."

We had Mom's infamous "stew," for dinner. She keeps a pot in the refrigerator. Practically everything we don't eat goes into that pot. When it's full, Mom pours on tomato sauce, heats it, and calls it "stew." Dad hates it and so do I. But Jeffrey doesn't care what we have for dinner. He hates everything that's not called "cookie" or "cake."

"You must eat three spoonfuls," Mom told Jeffrey.

I watched him. He ate three spoonfuls of tomato sauce. There wasn't a single hamburger bit, spinach leaf, chicken scrap, Brussels sprout, or lima bean in the sauce he ate, not even an elbow of macaroni.

I told Mom and Dad about Grams.

"Maybe she fell and hit her head," Mom said.

Mom also wondered what would happen with Sara while Grams was in the hospital. She said that a twelve-year-old couldn't be left alone. I hadn't thought about that. Mom said Sara could stay with us, that she could sleep in the living room. The couch there is a "convertible." We take off the pillows, pull it open, and it's a bed.

I nibbled on a lima bean and thought about watching the moving men, meeting Sara and Grams, shopping at Mr. Edwards's store, and then I remembered the counterfeit five-dollar bill. I told Dad about it.

"I had one yesterday at my store," Dad said. "Mrs. Andrews gave it to me."

Dad owns Benson's Variety. Plastered all over the front window of his store are signs like, Before You Look All Over Town, Look at Benson's, We Have It at Benson's, and Save Time. Save Money. Shop at Benson's.

"It wasn't a very good counterfeit bill," he added. "It was probably made on a copying machine. I didn't accept it, of course, but I wondered how Mrs. Andrews could have gotten it. If Grams had one, too, there must be a lot of them floating around. I'll have to be careful."

"T.F., would you like some more stew?"

"No, thank you."

"Good," Mom said as she poured the stew

from the bowl into the pot again. "There's enough left for tomorrow night."

Leftover leftovers! Yuck. Would Mom pour on *more* tomato sauce? Something had to be done.

"I changed my mind, Mom. I'll take some."

"I'll have an extra serving, too," Dad said.

"I knew you would. Today's stew was especially good, wasn't it?"

I didn't answer. Neither did Dad. I'm sure he took an extra serving because the thought of having stew two nights in a row was just too much. That's why I asked for more.

As I nibbled a hamburger bit, I wished we had a dog. Then I wouldn't have to eat this stuff. The dog would.

I also thought about Sara and Grams. I wondered what was happening at the hospital. I decided that right after dinner I would go downstairs and see if Sara had come home yet.

"Who wants dessert?" Mom asked. "We're having stewed fruit."

Mom doesn't throw anything out.

I helped Dad clear the table. Then I asked to be excused before dessert. "I want to see if Sara came back."

I walked down the two flights and knocked on 3D. I waited. I knocked again and waited, but no one came to the door.

Upstairs I helped Dad wash the dishes. While I was drying, he whispered to me, "Wasn't tonight's stew terrible?"

I nodded.

Then Dad said, "Let's try to finish everything Mom makes next week. Maybe we can avoid having stew for a while."

Dad talked all through cleanup. It was hard to hear what he was saying. The water was running, and I had to keep turning to put the dried dishes away. But I wasn't trying too hard to listen anyway. I was thinking about Grams and Sara. I couldn't imagine what was happening at the hospital.

"That's the last dish," Dad said. He shut off the water.

I dried the dish and put it away. I closed the cabinet door and turned around. Dad was looking at me.

"It's not like you to be so quiet, T.F. You usually talk and talk and talk. What's wrong?"

"I keep thinking about Grams going to the hospital."

"Oh," Dad said. He rubbed his nose. He does that sometimes when he thinks. "Hospitals can be scary places, but they don't have to be. It's the illnesses that are scary. A hospital is where you go to get better. Hospitals should be thought of like running into your parents' arms in the midst of a hurricane.''

"Dad," I said, "you should have been a poet."

"I know, but I like to play with all those cute little buttons on the cash register we have at the store."

He's such a tease.

I went to my room. I cleaned my desktop, sorted through the big middle drawer, and threw out some pens that didn't write and a few bent paper clips. And I kept looking out the window.

It was already past eight o'clock. Mom was trying to get Jeffrey into bed. He had taken a bath, brushed his teeth, and was in pajamas. Dad had read to him, but Jeffrey had only had three drinks of water, and Mom had only yelled at him twice. It would be at least another half hour and two more calls of "I'm untucked. Can you tuck me in again?" before he would be asleep. I wondered if I was like that when I was five.

I took out my baseball magazine and turned some pages. Then I saw a taxi cab drive up to our building. The back door opened, and an old woman got out. She looked somewhat familiar. Then someone else got out of the cab. First I saw her two socks, the red one and the white one. Then I saw her green plaid shorts and blue-striped shirt. Sara.

5. Aunt Rae, Blue Hair, and Fancy Jewelry

I ran from my room. I pressed the button for the elevator, and when it didn't come right away, I ran down the stairs. I met Sara in the lobby. The old woman from the taxi was with her. She wore a necklace, a dark blue skirt and jacket, and had blue-white hair. She was carrying a small suitcase.

"If you would get more exercise, you wouldn't be so out of breath," the woman told me.

"This is my friend, T.F. Benson," Sara told the woman, and then she told me, "This is my aunt Rae. She's Grams's sister."

That's why she looked so familiar to me. She

looked like Grams, except I couldn't imagine Grams with blue-white hair and dressing so fancy.

I asked Sara how Grams was feeling.

"She's better. The doctors think she had a small stroke."

"What's a stroke?"

Sara answered slowly. "The doctor told us that part of her brain was damaged because the flow of blood to the brain was interrupted."

"Oh."

"He thinks she will be fine, but they have to do some tests to make sure that's what she had. It could be a whole bunch of other things, but I don't remember what they are."

The elevator doors opened.

"Come, Sara," Aunt Rae said. "I have to get settled upstairs, and you have to change out of those ridiculous clothes."

Sara rolled her eyes up. Then, as the elevator doors were closing, she said, "T.F., meet me down here tomorrow morning at nine o'clock."

I stood there, wondering about Grams, the hospital, and Aunt Rae. Then I wondered why I was not on the elevator with them on my way to the fifth floor. I pressed the elevator button and waited for a moment. Then I decided to walk. The exercise would be good for me.

*   *   *

The next morning I was downstairs shortly after eight o'clock. Steve was washing our building's big front windows and the glass door. I helped him. I changed the water and carried the bucket to the sink when he finished. I helped him sweep the lobby, too.

Sara came down after nine. I hardly recognized her. Her hair was neatly combed. She was wearing a white blouse, a blue pleated skirt, white socks, and sneakers.

"Aunt Rae made me wear this," Sara said. "Aunt Rae told me that I had to wear 'normal' clothes or she wouldn't take me to visit Grams. She told me that too many stripes and plaids and polka dots would upset the other patients. But look," Sara said, and rolled down her socks.

Under her right sock was a green-and-yellow sock. Under her left sock was an orange-plaid sock. Under her blue skirt was a pair of red-and-purple-striped shorts.

Sara smiled at me and said, "A tiger can't change its spots."

"A leopard."

"Whatever."

The elevator doors opened again, and Aunt Rae got out. She smiled at me and said, "Good morning, B.F."

I didn't correct her.

"Doesn't Sara look nice this morning? Her Grams will be so pleased to see her dressed like a young lady."

I didn't tell her, but I thought Grams liked Sara to look and be different.

Sara said to me, "Please come with us. The hospital isn't far away. I don't know if they'll let you visit Grams, but you can wait for us in the lobby."

I hesitated. "I don't know."

"There will be lots of other people waiting in the lobby. You can talk to them. I know you'd like that."

Sara seemed really anxious for me to go along.

"I'll have to tell my mom," I said.

Sara went into the elevator with me. On the way up she said, "Aunt Rae keeps telling me how to dress and how to talk. She keeps trying to change me. Maybe with you along, she'll leave me alone."

I introduced Mom to Sara, and Mom seemed to like her, or maybe she liked the white blouse and blue skirt. I wished she could have seen what Sara was wearing when I first met her.

Anyway, Mom said I could go with Sara and Aunt Rae to the hospital.

On the way down Sara said, "I didn't tell you this before, but two years ago my parents both died in a car accident. Ever since then I have been a family project. Grams takes care of me, but everyone, especially Aunt Rae, tells her she's doing a lousy job of it. But I love my Grams. I don't think I could stand to live with anyone else."

When we came out of the elevator, Aunt Rae told us that she had just called for a taxi cab. Aunt Rae complained that the day before she had gone to the hospital by train, and it had taken her almost forty minutes. She lives near where Grams and Sara had lived before they moved. "Because there are three of us going today," she went on, "we'd each have to pay train fare. It will cost us about the same to take a taxi." Then she told us that it was a short ride to the hospital, and the cab would only charge us once for the ride even though there were three of us.

Aunt Rae seemed so different from Grams. If Grams wanted to take a cab, she would probably just say, "It will be fun."

It was a short drive to the hospital. When we got there, the meter read three dollars and something. Aunt Rae smiled as she gave the driver a five-dollar bill. "You can keep the change as a tip," she said.

"What do I look like, lady, some fool?" the driver snarled. "You can keep this money and give me some of the real stuff. This bill is as phony as your blue hair and your fancy jewelry."

6. A Suspect

"Oh my," Aunt Rae said. She took the five-dollar bill back from the cab driver and paid him again with different money.

As we walked into the hospital, Aunt Rae said, "I don't know what that man was talking about. I have real hair. I should have told him to pull it. And my necklace is real, too. The pearls aren't real, but it's still a real necklace."

Aunt Rae didn't say anything about the funny money, but that was all I was thinking about. I wondered who was passing it out.

The hospital lobby was crowded. People were reading, talking, going in and out of the gift shop, and walking past guards to the elevators. I found a seat near the windows. Aunt Rae let me look at the counterfeit bill while she and Sara went to visit Grams.

The green letters on the front of the bill were written by hand. President Lincoln's beard was fuzzy, and the paper didn't feel right. It looked just like the bill Sara had given Mr. Edwards.

I thought that it shouldn't be too hard to find who was passing these bills. Since Grams and Aunt Rae had each gotten one, all we had to do was check the places they went shopping. Whatever store both of them had shopped at was where they got the funny money. We could also speak to Mrs. Andrews, the lady who had given a funny bill to Dad.

I read once that detectives don't use guns much. Mostly they talk to people and ask questions. Maybe I'll be a detective when I finish school. I like to talk to people.

I glanced around the lobby. Some people looked worried, and some seemed relaxed. One man had two small children with him. He kept telling them to sit still and be quiet, but they didn't.

I got up and walked to the gift shop. I was looking at the candy rack when a man asked, "How old are you?"

"Twelve."

"My nephew is eleven. He just had his tonsils taken out. Would this be a good gift for him?"

The man showed me a stuffed animal, a green bird with a large yellow beak. I think it was a toucan.

"Don't give him that," I said. "He's almost twelve. Give him a sports magazine or a puzzle book."

Some people just don't realize that an eleven- or twelve-year-old is almost a teenager.

I was talking to the man and looking at the magazines he selected when Sara walked into the gift shop.

"Is this boy bothering you?" Sara asked the man.

"No," he said. He looked surprised.

"Good," Sara said. "T.F. loves to talk. Sometimes he talks too much."

"He was helping me," the man explained.

Then Sara said to me, "We have to go now."

I showed the man which magazines to buy. Then I followed Sara and Aunt Rae into a taxi cab. During the ride home Aunt Rae told me that Grams looked much better than the day before. Then she talked on and on again about what that first cab driver had said about her.

I tried to talk to Sara about the funny money. I told her that my dad had seen one of the counterfeit bills, too, and I thought we could find out who was passing them. "We know three people who were stuck with them. All we have to do is find out where they got their money."

Aunt Rae gently patted her hair. "I think this color looks good on me, don't you?" she asked Sara.

"I'll bet there's one store that *all* three of them went shopping in the last week," I said.

"These pearls may not be real, but they look nice."

I suggested, "We'll just make a list of where each person shopped and compare them."

Aunt Rae went on, "After all, why should I wear *real* pearls to a hospital?"

"Then we'll tell the police," I said.

"I have real pearls, too, you know."

Sara was having trouble listening to both of us at once, but I knew how to get her attention. "We're Super Kids. We could stand for justice, for truth, and for real money," I said, and stood up. I hit my head on the roof of the cab. I quickly sat down.

Aunt Rae was still talking about her necklace and hair. "The nurse said I looked real nice. She even complimented my dress and so did that nice man, Mr. Edwards."

"*Mr. Edwards!*" Sara and I both said it at the same time.

7. Lollipop, Lollipop, Grocery Man

We had arrived at our apartment building. Aunt Rae paid the driver and got out, but Sara and I just stared at each other.

"I can't believe it," I said. "I've known Mr. Edwards for years. He's always so nice to me."

Sara looked up, as if she knew some secret that I didn't know. "Sometimes criminals are the most innocent-looking people. Everyone likes them, but"—she bent forward, squinted her eyes at me, and continued—"but they're evil. They have a secret identity."

"Will you get out!" the cab driver almost shouted at us.

He was wearing big, dark sunglasses and had

bushy eyebrows. He was looking straight at us. He scared me.

"*Grrrr,*" Sara growled. Then we got out of the cab.

Sara told Aunt Rae that she would be up later. The two of us sat in the lobby and talked.

"I can't believe Mr. Edwards would do something like that," I insisted. "When I was young, he gave me a lollipop every time I came into his store."

Sara looked at me as if I were about two years old. Then she sang to the tune of "Pat-a-Cake, Pat-a-Cake":

> "*Lollipop, lollipop, grocery man,*
> *Make funny money as fast as you can,*
> *Print it and cut it and color it green,*
> *Give it to old women,*
> *Now aren't you mean?*"

"But he didn't give that phony bill to Grams," I told Sara. "*You* gave it to *him.*"

Sara thought for a moment, and I looked at her. She was still wearing the white blouse and blue skirt. She looked nice, but I didn't think she could ever get used to wearing what her aunt calls "normal" clothes.

"Mr. Edwards *said* I gave him that bill, but maybe I didn't. I only remember giving him two five-dollar bills. He took them. Then he showed me the funny money, made a red X on it, and gave it to us. Maybe he keeps a few phony bills in his cash register and sometimes pretends the customer gave one to him. That way he gets an extra five dollars. Other times, maybe, he waits to give funny money in change to someone in a hurry. Maybe he especially likes to give it to old women like Grams and Aunt Rae, because they don't see so well."

I thought about what Sara had said. She could have given him two real five-dollar bills, and then he could have switched one on us. It could have happened that way. We decided to go to the store and investigate. We'd watch as Mr. Edwards gave people their change.

"Do you have any money with you?" Sara asked me as we walked to the store.

I checked my pockets. I had seventy-eight cents.

When we walked into the store, Mr. Edwards asked us, "Can I help you?"

I didn't know what to answer, but Sara did.

"I'll pay you the five dollars I owe the next time I come here, but right now I have to get something for my aunt."

"What does she need?" Mr. Edwards asked.

"I don't know. She gave me seventy-eight cents to buy something, but I don't remember what it is."

"Maybe she needs onions."

"No."

"Milk?

"Yogurt?

"Tissues?

"Carrots?"

Sara shook her head and said, "No, none of those things. I'll just look around for a while. If I see it, I'll remember what it is."

Sara walked down the laundry-soap, toilet-tissue, and cat-food aisle.

"I know she's your friend," Mr. Edwards whispered to me, "but she's strange."

I thought Sara was smart. If she told him what Aunt Rae needed, we'd have to buy something, and we'd be out of the store in a few minutes. Now we could stay a really long time and watch Mr. Edwards give people change. And best of all, I could keep my seventy-eight cents.

I caught up with Sara in the cereal aisle. She was reading the nutritional information on a box of cornflakes.

We walked slowly through the store. Whenever someone came in and bought something, we watched him pay for it. The first two people didn't get much change, just a few coins. The third person paid for what he bought with the exact amount of money. He told Mr. Edwards he was trying to get rid of some pennies. Then an old man bought a carton of milk. He paid for it with a twenty-dollar bill. He got lots of change, including a five-dollar bill.

"Let's follow him," I whispered to Sara. "Maybe he has funny money in his change."

8. Wonderful Disguises

As we were on our way out of the store, Mr. Edwards stopped us.

"Did you find what you were looking for? Maybe your aunt wants salt. A big canister costs less than seventy-eight cents, or maybe she needs toothpicks, or a tomato, or a pint of milk."

"I'll have to ask her. I just can't remember. I just can't remember," Sara said as we left the store.

The old man was walking slowly. We ran and caught up with him near the bus stop.

"We know you just bought some milk," I said to him. "We'd like to see the change Mr. Edwards gave you."

The man looked at Sara, smiled, and began to walk away.

"We have to look at the money to see if it's real or not," I told him.

He turned, looked at us, and asked, "Are you thieves?"

"No. I'm T.F. Benson, and this is my friend Sara Bell. Sara's grandmother and Aunt Rae both got stuck with fake money, and we're trying to find out who gave it to them."

"We're investigating a crime," Sara said.

"Investigators?" the man said, looking a little confused as he took out his wallet. "Are you police officers in disguise? My, my, you look like children."

If he really thought we were police, he should have asked to see our badges. But he didn't. He just showed us the money he had in his wallet.

It all looked real to us. President Washington's and Alexander Hamilton's hair looked wavy and real. President Lincoln's beard didn't look at all fuzzy. The green numbers on all the bills were printed, not written by hand.

Sara returned the money to the man. She spoke to him in a deep, official-sounding voice, "Thank you for your cooperation. You can spend this money freely."

The man thanked us. He put his wallet in his

pocket, and as he slowly walked away, he said, "Wonderful disguises."

Sara must have known that I was thinking it proved Mr. Edwards was innocent, because she said, "This doesn't prove anything. Maybe he knew we were watching him."

The two of us quietly walked back toward Mr. Edwards's store. We live in a crowded neighborhood. There are apartment buildings and thousands of people living on every block. As we passed the underground-railway station, I recognized someone walking up the stairs. It was Mrs. Andrews.

I reminded Sara that Mrs. Andrews had given a phony bill to Dad. I had a pen with me. I gave Sara my seventy-eight cents, and she went into the stationery store to buy a memo pad so we could take notes.

"Hello, Mrs. Andrews," I called.

"Hello," she said, but she didn't seem to know who I was.

"I'm T.F. Benson," I explained. "I'm Jack Benson's son, of Benson's Variety. I've seen you in the store."

"Oh yes, you're the boy who talks so much. I was in a rush one day, and I made the mistake of asking you to show me where the pens were. You told me about click pens and stick pens and roller-ball pens and fountain pens and erasable pens. I left your father's store with a terrible headache and without a pen."

"Yes, I remember. My father doesn't let me talk to customers anymore. When they ask me for something, I just point."

Mrs. Andrews started to walk away.

"No, wait. I want to talk to you."

Sara came out of the stationery store. I introduced her to Mrs. Andrews. Sara opened the memo pad to take notes.

"We heard that you got stuck with a phony five-dollar bill," I said. "Sara's grandmother and her aunt Rae did, too. We want to catch the counterfeiter, and it would help if we knew where you've shopped in the past few days, where you might have gotten the phony money."

"Hmm," she replied. "I bought a dress at Miller's, a pair of shoes at Walking Tall, and a newspaper at the newsstand, but I didn't get change there. I paid exactly what the newspaper cost."

Sara wrote "newsstand" in the memo pad anyway.

"I picked up some things at A and B Cleaners. I shopped at Mr. Edwards's store, and I went to Benson's."

"Thank you, Mrs. Andrews," Sara said. "We'll call you if we find the counterfeiter."

I thanked her, too, and told her she looked

really nice in her dress. I asked her if it was the dress she'd bought at Miller's; did it seem that my father needed help in the store; and if she thought it would rain. The weatherman had said it would, but I didn't see many clouds.

"I'm sorry, T.F.," she said, "I have to go now. Suddenly I have a headache."

After she left, Sara and I looked at the list.

"I know who's passing the funny money," I told Sara.

And Sara said, "So do I."

Mrs. Andrews
Miller's
Walking Tall
Newsstand
A and B Cleaners
Mr. Edwards's
Benson's

9. Something Is Afoot

Sara pointed to the fifth item on the list, Mr. Edwards's grocery. She gave me the memo pad, and I pointed to the fourth item, the A and B Cleaners.

"It's a big cleaning store," I said. "Lots of people go there, and they are always in a hurry. The only way anyone could pass one of these lousy bills is by giving it to someone who is in too much of a rush to look at his change."

Sara shrugged. "We'll get a list from Aunt Rae of the places she went shopping. Tomorrow when I visit Grams I'll talk to her, too."

She paused for a moment. She looked down and said, "When I saw her this morning, I didn't know what to say. She was in bed with tubes attached to her, and she couldn't talk. I was scared. Aunt Rae told me to cheer up Grams, tell her what I'm doing, but I had nothing to say. I just held her hand."

Sara looked up. "Tomorrow I'll have something to tell her. I'll talk about Mr. Edwards, Mrs. Andrews, and our plan to find out who's passing the funny money. Then, even if she can't speak, maybe she can point to the places on our list where she shopped."

I told Sara it was getting late. It was past lunchtime. My mother and Aunt Rae would be wondering where we were. We decided to walk toward home when I saw someone leave Mr. Edwards's store. Mr. Edwards!

"That's odd," I whispered to Sara. "When we were there, no one else was working in the store. He can't just leave. My father would never leave Benson's in the middle of the day."

We watched Mr. Edwards close the door and lock it. He taped up a sign, Sorry. We're Closed. We'll Be Back Soon. Then he walked off.

"Let's follow him," Sara whispered. "Something is afoot."

Mr. Edwards didn't look at all suspicious to me. Maybe Sara was right. Maybe I'm not a good judge of people. Or maybe she's wrong, and he's a nice, honest, lollipop-giving man, just as I have always thought he was.

"Shh," Sara whispered. "We can't let Mr. Edwards know we're following him."

He walked quickly down the block, waited at the corner, and then crossed the street. I started to follow him.

"No, not yet," Sara said. "We don't want to be too close."

Mr. Edwards was halfway down the next block before Sara said we should go. We waited at the corner for a large moving truck to ride past. It blocked our view. Then he was gone.

10. Look, Green Ink!

Sara and I ran across the street.

"He couldn't have reached the corner yet," I said. "He must have gone into one of the stores."

We raced down the block to where we had last seen Mr. Edwards. There were lots of places he could have gone. There were doors leading to offices and apartments upstairs, and there was a line of stores. One of them was A and B Cleaners. We went in there.

A man dropped an armload of clothes onto the counter, and a woman working there threw them one by one into a bin. She gave the man a receipt and told him he could pick up his clothes on Friday.

Behind the counter there were bins, mechanized clothes racks, and way in the back of the shop, I saw people working with large pressing machines. I didn't see Mr. Edwards.

"Can I help you?" the woman asked us.

Sara said, "We're just looking."

"There's nothing to look at here. Either you have dirty clothes for us to clean, or you've come to pick some clothes up."

"Oh."

"This is not a tourist attraction. People don't come in here just to look."

We left A and B and walked into the beauty parlor next door.

"Do you have an appointment?" a woman asked us.

Sara answered, "No, we're just looking."

"We give the latest cuts. You could even show us a picture of what you want, and we can do it."

Sara said, "Thank you."

"Of course, you can't come in here with short hair and show us a picture of someone with a ponytail. We can't make your hair longer."

Mr. Edwards wasn't in there either. We walked into the drugstore.

"Hello, T.F. Hello, Sara."

It was Mr. Edwards. He was going out when we walked in. He was carrying something in a small paper bag. Once he had walked past, Sara discreetly pointed at him and nodded.

"No," I said, "he's not the one. He can't be printing funny money. He's so friendly, and my parents have known and trusted him for a long time."

"I think you're wrong, T.F., and here's the proof." Sara pointed to a rack of pens and said, "Look, green ink."

I know I like people and always try to think the best of everyone, but surely anyone could see that this wasn't real evidence. Sara wanted to convict this man, to send him to prison as a counterfeiter, because he had just left a store that sells green pens.

On our way back to our building, I told Sara, "You have a great imagination, but you're a lousy detective."

"Oh, don't muffle your feathers. I haven't sent him to jail yet. I just think he's acting suspicious."

"Ruffle. Don't ruffle your feathers."

"Whatever."

"I think we have to do more investigating," I said. "We have to speak to more people and ask more questions of everyone we know who got some of the funny money."

We were walking past the bus stop outside our

apartment building when we saw Aunt Rae coming toward us. She was walking fast and she was angry.

"So this is where I find you. Do you know what time it is? Do you know that your lunch has been on the table for almost an hour? Do you know I have been worried about you?"

Aunt Rae didn't give Sara a chance to answer any of her questions. I walked with them into the building. Aunt Rae pressed the button for the elevator. While we waited, Sara saw her own reflection in the mirror.

"Yuck! Look at what I'm wearing!"

"You look nice," Aunt Rae told her.

"Nice! I look like an old blue penguin; a bluebird with socks on; a blue pleated convertible with whitewall tires; an elephant in a tutu . . . I look terrible."

The elevator doors opened. We all got on.

"Wait! Stop, T.F.!" I heard someone shout. "Don't go up yet."

11. I've Got It! I've Got It!

Steve was waving some paper and calling to me. I got off the elevator and went to him. The paper was a five-dollar bill. I didn't have to look too carefully to know it was fake.

"Where did you get it?" I asked him.

"Do you think I know that?" he answered. "I'm sure I didn't have it in my wallet when I left this morning, and now here it is."

The elevator door had closed. Sara was on her way upstairs.

"I'd like to ask you some questions," I told Steve.

I took out the pen and memo pad so I could

take notes. Then Steve told me where he had gone shopping earlier in the day.

"I needed money this morning, so I went to the bank and made a withdrawal. Then I bought a hammer at the hardware store, a newspaper, and a watchband at Jackson Jewelers. I took the train to school and bought the books I'll need for the next semester. I ate lunch in the school cafeteria. I paid for that, too."

I made a list of every place Steve spent money.

"I always look at my change and count it," he

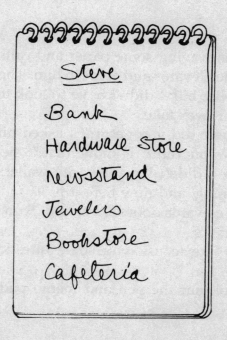

said. "I don't know how I could have gotten stuck with this."

I thanked Steve, and then I went upstairs to 3D. Sara came to the door. "Aunt Rae is happy now," she whispered. "She thinks I'm undernourished, and every time I eat another forkful of noodles, she smiles."

I told Sara about Steve and showed her the list I had made while speaking to him. We compared it with the one from Mrs. Andrews. Only the newsstand matched, and Mrs. Andrews had said she didn't get any change there. Then we asked Aunt Rae who might have given her the fake five-dollar bill.

"I'm usually careful with money, but your grandmother's illness distracted me. I've been so upset, I don't know who gave me that money."

I looked at the lists we had from Mrs. Andrews and Steve and started to question Aunt Rae. "Have you bought anything at Miller's? Walking Tall?"

"No."

"I know you shop at Mr. Edwards's store."

"Yes, I have a friend who lives nearby. I shop at Mr. Edwards's store whenever I'm in the neighborhood. Mr. Edwards is always so friendly."

"Do you go to A and B Cleaners?"

"No."

"Jackson Jewelers?"

"No."

"The hardware store?"

"Of course not. What would I buy at a hardware store?"

"Did you buy anything at the newsstand?"

"No."

I didn't ask if she went to the Fillmore College bookstore or cafeteria. I didn't think she did. And I didn't ask if she shopped at Dad's store. I know he's not a counterfeiter.

Of course, there could be more than one person passing the phony money. It could also be passed from one person to the next. What if Dad hadn't looked at the money Mrs. Andrews gave him and then he spent it somewhere?

"I'll visit Grams tomorrow," Sara said. "Maybe she'll remember where she went shopping."

That night at dinner we had fish sticks, mashed potatoes, and broccoli. Dad and I made sure to finish the potatoes. We didn't want them in Mom's leftover stew. We'd had them in the stew once before, and with tomato sauce on top, they looked like red mud and tasted even worse.

The next morning I met Sara and Aunt Rae downstairs. Sara was wearing a yellow blouse and green pants. Her clothing was more colorful than what she'd worn the day before, but not nearly like what she'd worn the day I met her.

"I'm giving the plaids and stripes a rest," she told me.

We went together to the hospital. Aunt Rae and Sara spoke to the guard there. Then they came back and said I could go in with them to visit Grams.

I was nervous about seeing Grams. This was the first time I'd been in a hospital room since I was born. I certainly don't remember what it was like then. I was only three days old when Mom took me home.

In the elevator there was a man holding a large bunch of blue balloons with It's a Boy! printed on them. There were also two doctors. I knew they were doctors because they had stethoscopes in their pockets.

We got off on the fifth floor. I followed Aunt Rae and Sara down the hall. Some of the doors to the hospital rooms were open, and I saw people lying in bed. Some had visitors. A few were sleeping, and most of the others were watching television.

Grams smiled when we came in, but she didn't say anything. Aunt Rae talked to her first. She told her all about Sara, what she ate, and asked, "Doesn't she look nice?"

Grams smiled again.

Her smile was different from the way it was the first time I met her. It seemed crooked. She was pale, and there was a tube going into her arm.

Aunt Rae told her, "Sara can be disciplined. She just needs a strong hand. For lunch she ate a big plate of egg noodles, and for dinner she had lots of carrots, meatballs, and spaghetti. I don't let her eat any cake or candy until after she has finished her dinner. And I don't let her wear all those horrible clothes. All those stripes and plaids might affect her personality. Solid colors will calm her."

Then Sara walked near the bed and whispered to Grams, "I hate these clothes."

Grams reached for Sara's hand, held it, and smiled.

Sara told Grams all about the funny money. She told her that we were trying to find the counterfeiter. Sara asked her if she had shopped at any of the places on our lists. Grams nodded only once, when Sara pointed to "Hardware Store."

I was shocked. There was not one store that everyone had shopped at. I had been so sure we would solve this mystery once we'd spoken to all the people with the counterfeit bills. But I was wrong.

Sara and Aunt Rae talked in the taxi cab during the whole ride home. I was too upset even to listen.

All I could think about was giving up my plan to become a detective.

When we got close to our building, I saw Mr. Edwards's store and all the others on the block. I saw someone stop on his way to the train station to buy a newspaper, and suddenly I grabbed Sara's arm and said, "I've got it! I've got it! I know who has been passing those bills!"

12. Who Is It?
Who Is It?

The cab had stopped in front of our building. Aunt Rae paid the driver and waited for a moment. I think she expected him to say something about the money and maybe even about her hair and jewelry.

"So who is it? Who is it?" Sara asked as we walked into the building.

Steve was in the lobby. He opened the door for us and asked Aunt Rae, "How is Grams?"

"Better," she answered. "She may come home soon. But she'll have to go back to the hospital a few times a week for speech and physical therapy."

Sara sat next to me on the couch in the lobby and asked again, "So who is it?"

"I'm going upstairs now," Aunt Rae told her. "You can stay here with your friend, but don't leave the building."

Aunt Rae got onto the elevator, and I asked Sara, "Do you know why everyone has a different list of places they shopped at?"

"No."

"It's because people go to this place so often, they don't even remember getting change there."

"Will you tell me where it is already! The suspense is filling me."

"You mean 'killing me.'"

"Whatever."

"It must be the newsstand," I said. "People go there all the time. Buying a newspaper is not something people really think about, but they do it. They spend money there and get change."

"But Grams didn't go to the newsstand," Sara reminded me. "We asked her that. And neither did Aunt Rae."

I sat there for a while and thought. I didn't say anything at all, and that's not easy for me. I thought about when Mr. Edwards first told us the money was counterfeit and about all the other funny money. I remembered asking Mrs. Andrews where she went shopping, and then I remembered that I saw her coming up from the underground train station. She had told us that she bought a paper, but she'd paid for it with the exact change.

I remembered when we took the cab to the hospital and the driver told Aunt Rae that her money was fake. I remembered, too, that Aunt Rae complained that it had taken her so long to get to the hospital that first day, and I remembered how Steve gets to school.

All at once it dawned on me. "I really have it now," I told Sara. "I know who's been passing the funny money."

"Is it the bank?"

"Of course not. They're trained to look at money carefully. They wouldn't pass counterfeit bills."

"Mr. Edwards?"

"No. Steve didn't shop there. But there is one place Grams, Aunt Rae, Mrs. Andrews, and Steve all spent money. They all rode on the train."

Sara looked at me. Then she said, "We don't have a car. Grams takes the train when she goes to work. We even rode on the train when we moved from our old apartment to this one."

"You didn't ride for free," I told her. "You had to buy a token. It's not something you think about buying, but you *do* buy it, and unless you pay the exact amount, you get change."

"Let's ask Steve," Sara said.

We found him in the laundry room.

"Steve," Sara asked, "did you buy a train token yesterday?"

"I must have. I rode the train to school," Steve said, and then he thought for a moment. "I remember now. I gave the clerk a ten-dollar bill and asked for two tokens. He gave them to me along with the change and said, 'You better hurry. The train is coming into the station.'"

"What did you do?" I asked.

"I hurried, of course, but when I got downstairs, there was no train."

"What did you do with the change the clerk gave you?"

"I must have put it in my pocket, but I was in such a hurry, I don't remember."

Steve sat next to us and said, "That must be when I got the phony bill."

"Aunt Rae rode on the train to the hospital the first time she went to visit Grams," Sara said.

"We should call the police," I said.

Steve told us to wait for that. "There are lots of token clerks. Before we tell anyone, I want to be sure of the one who gave me the phony bill."

I stood up and said, "Let's go to the train station and see which clerk is working there."

First Sara had to tell Aunt Rae. "She'll swallow a cow if she comes downstairs and I'm not here," she explained.

We promised to wait for her.

While she was upstairs, Steve said, "I hope I recognize the clerk. They sit in a closed booth, and I really didn't get a very good look at him."

Sara came down and we walked to the station. Steve told us that when we got downstairs, we should pretend we were waiting for someone. Otherwise the clerk would know we were watching him.

The train runs under the street. Near the bottom of the stairs is a token booth. Before you can get on a train, you need to buy a token at the booth, drop it into the turnstile coin slot, and walk down some more stairs onto the platform.

The station is very crowded in the morning, when people rush to work, and it gets crowded again in the late afternoon, when they come home. Often there is a long line of people waiting to buy tokens. But when we got there, it was about eleven-thirty in the morning. The station was not busy at all.

We stood near the token booth. Steve looked at the clerk. He was sitting on a high stool, so we couldn't see how tall he was, but even sitting down, he looked fat. He had a large droopy mustache and was wearing a blue baseball cap. Steve whispered to us, "It's him."

We had finally found our man. I had read somewhere that detectives must be patient. Well, now I knew it was true.

"Let's watch and see if he passes any more funny money," I suggested.

Steve told us to keep looking around as if we were waiting for someone. I looked around a little, but Sara became almost frantic. She was unbelievable. She kept calling out, "Where is she? Where is she? Where is Aunt Sadie?"

Steve told her to stop. She may be a good artist, but she's a lousy actress.

A man came into the station, but he didn't buy a token. He already had one, which he dropped into the token slot. Then he pushed the turnstile and went to the platform to wait for the next train. Another man came in and bought a token, but he only got a few coins—no bills—in change.

A few minutes later a woman headed for the booth. She took a bill from her purse. "Two please," she said to the token clerk. He gave her the tokens and some bills and coins in change.

"I have to speak to her. I have to find out if she got a phony bill," Steve whispered.

The woman had gone through the turnstile. "Now I'll have to buy a token to speak to her," Steve said. He quickly bought one and followed her downstairs onto the platform.

While Sara and I waited, we heard the rumbling of a train entering the station. We couldn't see the platform, but we heard the doors open and someone say, "Please watch your step getting off the train," and, "Stand clear of the closing doors." Then we heard the rumbling of the train as it left the station.

Some people came through the exit gate, but not Steve. We waited for a while, but it was obvious that he wasn't coming out.

"He must have followed the woman onto the train," I whispered.

Sara looked at her watch. It was twelve o'clock. "I have to get home for lunch. Aunt Rae told me not to be late."

Just then a man with a large set of keys unlocked the door to the token booth and went inside. The clerk there spoke to him and then left the booth and walked to the stairs.

"He's leaving. What do we do now?" Sara asked.

We watched him walk up the stairs. He was wearing white pants, sneakers, and a bright red shirt, and he was carrying a brown paper bag.

"He's probably going for a lunch break," I whispered. "Let's follow him."

This was real detective stuff. We went quickly up the stairs. The clerk was walking toward a small park I used to go to when I was much younger. It has a few swings, a slide, a sandbox, and some benches. "That bag is probably filled with funny money," I whispered.

"Don't jump to delusions," Sara replied.

"Conclusions."

"Whatever," she said, and she didn't whisper it.

The man turned and looked straight at us. Then he went into the park and sat on one of the benches. I was sure he knew we were following him.

"We can't just sit and watch what he does," I told Sara. "We have to do something. Let's go on the swings."

Sara looked at me again, as she had when she'd first noticed my clothes matched. But that's what we did. We each sat on one of the swings, and I started to pump. I went really high and pretended to enjoy myself. Actually it *was* fun.

We watched the man open the brown bag. He took out a sandwich and a large cookie, not money. He stretched out his legs and started to eat. I had expected him to lead us to some dark hangout where we'd need a secret password to get in and where printing presses were rolling out more and more funny money. But there he was, calmly eating his lunch.

I stopped pumping. "Let's go," I told Sara.

When we were outside the park, I said, "I don't think he's the one. All he's doing is eating."

"Of course he's eating," Sara said. "Even counterfeiters get hungry."

I thought about what Sara had said, but still, the clerk didn't seem guilty to me. I was all out of ideas. I decided again that detective work wasn't for me.

We walked slowly toward our building. Just as we were passing the entrance to the train station, Steve came running up the stairs. When he saw us, he said, "He's gone. The clerk isn't in the token booth anymore, but he's the one passing the phony bills. The train came before I could speak to the woman, so I had to get on. She was still holding her change, and in it was a phony five-dollar bill. She said it was the second one she got this week."

"Yes!" I shouted. "I am a detective!"

Then I told Steve, "I know where the clerk is. He's in the park eating lunch."

We had to almost run to keep up with Steve. But when we got to the park, the clerk in the red shirt was gone.

13. All's Swell

"He was right here," I said.

I sat on the same bench the clerk had been on just a few minutes before. I mimicked what he had done. I opened an imaginary paper bag, took out an imaginary sandwich and cookie, and pretended to eat. After two bites of the sandwich, I reached for something and it wasn't there, not even in my imagination.

"He's thirsty. He went for something to drink," I said.

Steve looked at me in amazement and asked, "Did you see him? Did he just walk past?"

"I didn't see him," I said, "but if I was eating a sandwich and a dry cookie, I'd need a drink."

Sara nodded. She agreed with me.

There was a small candy shop near the entrance to the park. As we started to walk toward it, we saw the clerk coming out carrying an open can of soda.

After that everything happened quickly. Steve sent me to call the police. For the first twelve years of my life I had never called 911. Now, within just a few days, I had called it twice.

I made the call from the nearest public telephone. While I answered the operator's questions, I watched Steve and Sara follow the clerk. At first he was just walking along slowly, but then he turned and saw Steve and Sara following him. He walked faster, and then he ran. Steve took off after him. Sara couldn't keep up. I got off the telephone and met Sara near the entrance to the train station. We went downstairs and met Steve right outside the token booth.

The clerk was inside, looking out at Steve through the metal bars and thick glass window. The clerk looked angry.

"I don't think he knows why I ran after him," Steve said. "He ran into the booth, locked the door, and then called someone on the telephone. I'll bet he thinks I was trying to rob him and called the police."

"Maybe he knows why you were chasing

him," I said, "and decided to call some of his criminal friends."

Steve said, "I didn't think of that."

Sara wanted to leave, but I told her we couldn't do that. We had called the police, and we should wait for them.

Two city police came down the stairs as two policemen who worked for the subway system got off an incoming train. The token clerk came out from the booth.

"This man was threatening me," the clerk said, and pointed to Steve.

"That's ridiculous. I wasn't threatening anyone. I was chasing him because he gave me this." Steve took the fake five-dollar bill from his pocket and showed it to the policemen. "I bought tokens yesterday, and he gave it to me in my change."

"Let me see that," one of the policemen said.

The token clerk started to run. The two train police went after him. When they came back, they had the clerk with them. His wrists were locked in handcuffs.

"What's the fuss?" the clerk asked. "It's only five dollars. I'll give the man his money back."

I think Steve might have been happy with that, but one of the police officers said, "Passing counterfeit money is against the law. That's the fuss."

We watched the police take the clerk away.

Later Steve told us that following the man wasn't too smart. The counterfeiter could have had a weapon. He could have gotten violent. But he didn't. Steve said he followed him without thinking about what might happen because he was angry. He worked hard for his money, and he didn't like being stuck with the counterfeit bill.

I found out everything else I know about what happened by reading the newspaper. The police searched the booth, the clerk, and his apartment. They found about fifty phony bills, a copying machine, and lots of green pens. The clerk kept the counterfeit bills beneath the counter in the token booth. He gave them only to people who were in too much of a rush to catch a train to look carefully at their change.

A few days later a reporter asked Steve, Sara, and me to meet her at the police station. A photographer took our picture. It appeared in the newspaper, too. Mom and Dad were really proud of me. Jeffrey said that in the picture my hair looked funny.

"All's swell that ends swell," Sara said when I showed her and Steve the article.

"It's well," I said. "All's well that ends well."

"Whatever."

"It's not so swell," Steve said. "I'm still stuck with a phony five-dollar bill."

But I knew Steve was pleased. He taped copies of the article and the photograph on the mirror next to the elevator, where everyone would see them.

14.   Let's Party!

The best news for Sara that week was that Grams would be coming home. "She won't be able to go back to work," Sara told me. "And she'll need therapy to learn to talk clearly and to walk, but she's coming home."

Mom said we should make some big signs to welcome her back. We made them in my apartment because even though Mom hates a mess, she doesn't hate it nearly as much as Aunt Rae does. Anyway, it was Mom's suggestion.

First we went to Dad's store. Sara had a long list of the things she needed: large sheets of oak tag, colored construction paper, markers, glue, foam, something plaid, and tissues.

Mom covered the kitchen table and floor with newspaper. She brought us a large bag for garbage. Then she asked Sara, "What will you write on the signs?"

"How about, Welcome Home, I'm Glad You Are Better, and Take It Easy?" Sara suggested.

"That's nice," Mom said.

Sara smiled, but it was a strange smile, not the sort I would trust.

We all helped her make the signs. Sara had a list of letters she needed: *A A A A A B C D E E E E E E E E F I I I I K L L L M M M N O O O O O P R R S T T T T U U V W Y Y Y* and *Z*.

Jeffrey picked the colors, and we cut them out of construction paper.

Mom kept telling Sara that the list was wrong. "You're missing an *H* for 'Home' and the *G* for 'Glad', and there are a few extra letters."

Sara just told us to keep cutting, so we did. When Sara started to paste the letters onto the oak tag, I thought Grams might have to start a new book, *Sara's Book of Peculiar Signs*.

With the cutout letters Sara spelled Welcome Foam on the first sign. Beneath that she pasted a small piece of foam rubber. On the second sign she spelled I Am Plaid You Are Better and pasted on plaid wrapping paper. She stapled a few tissues on the third sign and spelled Take It Sneezy.

There was one sheet of oak tag left. Sara wrote on it, ☀ ♡ ∪ !   and beneath that (I Love You!)

"Now that's a nice sign," Mom said.

"They're all nice," I said. "Grams will like them."

I helped Sara tape the signs to the front door of her apartment and to the walls of the kitchen.

"The tape will take the paint off," Aunt Rae said.

"I have a paint set," Sara told her aunt. "If some paint comes off the door or the wall, I'll re-paint it."

"I know all about your paints. Imagine, paint-ing a whole door purple. Don't you paint this door purple. The landlord will throw you out of the building."

Then Aunt Rae read the signs.

"And what does Welcome Foam mean? I'm Plaid You Are Better is silly. If you want Grams to get better, you'll stop wearing plaids. All those colors will only upset her. Take It Sneezy. That's ridiculous! Your grandmother needs rest, not non-sense!"

Aunt Rae didn't say anything about the last sign. I'm not sure she could read the rebus, but I know she understood the I Love You part. She knew Sara really loves Grams. Sara and Grams had their own special way of communicating, and I think Aunt Rae was jealous.

After we were all done taping the signs to the door and walls, Aunt Rae said, "If you insist on putting up all these silly signs and making such a fuss, maybe we should have a little party."

We called my father at the store and asked him to bring home some balloons and streamers. Then Aunt Rae told us to go to Mr. Edwards's store and buy some cake and other goodies.

"I still owe him five dollars," Sara said.

Aunt Rae gave Sara the money, and we went to the store.

"I saw your picture in the newspaper," he said when we came in. "Congratulations."

I was about to tell him that he had been a suspect, but I didn't. I didn't think he would like to hear that. Instead I looked at more pictures of his granddaughter and told him how cute she is.

Mr. Edwards told me he had not been able to visit her lately. His wife had been sick. The doctor said she had the flu. Mr. Edwards told me he had had to close the store a few times to get medicine and bring it to her. That must be what he had been doing when Sara and I saw him coming out of the drugstore.

Sara bought a cake at Mr. Edwards's and lots of chocolate goodies. She paid Mr. Edwards for everything, including the five dollars she owed him.

I sat by my bedroom window the next morning and waited for Sara, Grams, and Aunt Rae to come home from the hospital. As soon as I saw the cab, I ran out of the apartment. The elevator was waiting at our floor, and I was about to get on, but I quickly changed my mind. I decided to race it down, just as I had the first day I met Sara and Grams. I stuck my hand inside the elevator, pressed 1, and ran to the stairs. I got down really fast, before the elevator, and even before Sara, Grams, and Aunt Rae got into the building.

Aunt Rae held the door open. Grams was in a wheelchair. Sara pushed it into the building. It was the *old* Sara, the one I'd met when she first moved into the building. She was wearing a red-and-white-striped shirt, purple plaid shorts, and socks that didn't match. I don't mean that they didn't match the shorts and the shirt. They didn't match each other. One was yellow and the other was white with pink hearts.

Grams waved to me as she came in. I smiled. It was good to have her back. It was time to party.

ABOUT THE AUTHOR

DAVID A. ADLER has written many books for children, including *The Dinosaur Princess and Other Prehistoric Riddles*, and the Cam Jansen mysteries. He lives in New York with his wife and family.